(Chapter 1)

(The Demon's Domain)

The sun set as Tracey pulled into the last lot of the dead end street. She was on the very back end of the farm now. It was very spooky and scary as all hell actually. She really wasn't sure about this trip. But she would be comfortable when everyone else finally had arrived. She was still awaiting on several other teammates to show up. They had not yet arrived. And she was really hoping someone would show up soon.

Finally two other cars had now shown up. And everyone was already drinking and partying as they all jumped out of their cars. Jumping around and acting crazy, her friends all formed a circle as they all celebrated their arrival. They all raised their beers and toasted each other. Yelling and screaming as they carried on like the maniacs they were.

The farm was well over two thousand acres. Only five acres of that were where the farm and the Stables and the Barn as well. All together had filled the void. The owners were out of town and had left the property to Tracey. In order for her team to do their weekend investigation of the property itself. They had been ran off of their property by some sort of spirit. A very wicked Demon the father had reported to the police.

The Demon had already been present. When the family had moved there in the first place. But it had been without any doubt scary as hell and the farmers wife had demanded they leave. Furniture had been launched allover the house at times. Books would fly off of the bookshelf out of nowhere. And at times they would end up in areas allover the house. Without any explanation at all.

The team had all arrived Thursday. The plan had been to kick back and cut loose on the first night. Then spend Friday, Saturday and Sunday doing a serious full on investigation of the property. No retreat no surrender was the whole teams mindset. The team would all unpack the rest of the gear and get it into the house and upon doing so set it up and start immediately. Tracey changed the plan in that moment it was a go.

(Chapter 2)

(The Demon's Domain)

The cameras were now running in each and every room of the house. The crew had all gathered outside just the four of them. The team was formed of three men and woman. Tracey being the only woman involved. But still yet the most experienced in the field. The men were used in the field mostly for protection. And to set up the equipment upon their arrival. And to also pack it up and get it ready for travel at the end of the mission.

They were experienced in the field for the most part. But even with all of the expertise in the field. It was still dangerous as hell to get involved with the supernatural in any way shape or form. The spirits and demons that had been summoned up and or cast out were powerful to say the very least. Each investigation had to be thoroughly done.

If not the Spirits and or demons would come back and the scary part was that. They could be twice as powerful. Maybe even so powerful that their would be no chance of expelling them from the farm the house. So with the description of these Demons that had been described to her. Tracey knew she would have to be very careful. In trying to rid the property of this evil.

There was now a bad storm moving onto the farm land. And for the most part would most likely mess with the equipment. So the crew would probably have to wait out the storm. Before actually turning on the cameras to record any evidence. The team which consisted of two brothers. Mike and Arron that were both well educated in the field of Poltergeists and Hauntings anything Paranormal for that matter.

Then their was Sims, who was actually educated in most every subject related to the paranormal field. And also amazing at anything tech as well. He was a very courageous individual to say the least. And then their was Tracey who was just like Sims. Not afraid of anything. And very educated in the field of the Paranormal. Pretty much an expert with her experience in the field.

(Chapter 3)

(The Demon's Domain)

Once the crew had gathered all of the equipment from out of the van. The brought it into the front living room. And place it on the table. The tri-pods were staged on the floor. Standing in their upright position. The team now set on the couch and in chairs. As they planned this next investigation one last time. Going over the very basics again.

Tracey immediately warned the others that this wasn't any regular investigation. That from what she'd been told. This presence was that of a very strong and determined demon or spirit. And it had already managed to force the whole family to leave. The team took the warning seriously. They never fooled around with their work. Always taking it as serious as possible.

All of a sudden their was a flash of lightning from just outside of the front window. In that moment the back screen door had opened and then slammed shut from the wind of the incoming storm. Then out of nowhere the front door opened up as if someone had just walked in. Suddenly after a few seconds of standing there. The crew aged ten years in that moment. From what they'd all just witnessed.

The front door slammed shut just as fast as it had opened. The lights going out in the whole house at that very same moment. The crew all took a deep breath. As if they'd known not to show fear in any way at all what so ever. They all joined in a circle together. Heading towards the front door of the house. Without a doubt in shock, each and every one of them.

Suddenly as the group had hit the front room to the door. The lights came back on in a flash. The group all exhaled letting out a deep breath of air, as they now felt so relieved that they could once again see clearly. In that moment a book came flying off of the book shelf from the side of the room. As it hit Sims in the legs and then dropped on the floor right at his feet.

He looked down to take a glance at the book. Unsure if it would fly up and hit him in the face. He then reached down and picked the book up. As he brought it towards his body to look at the cover. The cover read ; Hauntings And Strange Happenings In Ohio. He dropped the book instantly. Running towards the front door as his legs were swept out immediately from up under his feet.

Sims layed there, unsure of how to react to what had just taken place ? he thought. As he stared over at Tracey as she said to him quickly. "Stay calm" "this shall soon pass". Sims now lay there at the front door. Scared as stiff as a board and not moving a muscle. The group waited for a few minutes. To see what would happen next. And if so who would be attacked.

(Chapter 4)

(The Demon's Domain)

Nothing else happened and things seemed to calm down. If even for a few moments it would gladly be accepted. As the team was clearly shaken up badly. Tracey knew in that moment exactly why the family had fled their comforts of their own home. She said to the group in a calm tone. "Team we have to tread lightly". "That's all I want to say". "I hope you all understand what it is that I am saying to you".

The group all nodded their heads without saying a word one. Sims now got back up onto his feet as he trembled. Trying to stop his body from shaking so immensely. He then said quickly and in a low tone. "Let's go back outside and re-group". Tracey instantly replying with a quick "No". "If we do that it shows fear". "And their power grows stronger in that moment".

Leaving Sims disappointed as he lowered his head in defeat at that exact moment. He then replied back to Tracey. "Well" "will they hear anything that we talk about and are trying to plan Tracey" ? he asked. "It isn't a Debate" Tracey answered back. "We have to get all of these cameras on". "We've already missed so much evidence" and video proof of It all to boot".

"It's time we get our asses together and really get this investigation going". The group moved towards the equipment with a short burst of energy. Unpacking and placing all of the cameras on top of the tripods. Immediately turning them on. "Now we're a go". Tracey said happily she was full of energy and newly found excitement that energized her.

The storm was now over the top of the House and the rain started to pour down. With flashes of lightning almost every ten seconds. Their was now a whole new feeling of fear overwhelming the team. Tracey knew that this wasn't good at all. She shouted out in an instant as she lashed out at her friends. "Rock Up". "And Get your shit together right now people" "Remember", "Your Professionals".

(Chapter 5)

(The Demon's Domain)

The group took a few minutes now to gather up enough courage. To gain some composure in order to push forward and continue the mission at hand. They had to gather up enough proof for a documentary film. And as well in finishing have a priest come and bless the home itself. Hopefully cleansing the space once and for all. Any evil that dwelled within the house and around its premises.

The Night went on as the team pushed on Placing cameras on tri-pods and setting them up within the rooms of the house. The storm continued to ramble on. It's fury growing over time as it seemed to loom over top of the entire property. Nobody had been attacked in a couple of hours. But they knew that it was still early and that an attack could happen at any time.

Most often these paranormal situations would occur late at night or in the early morning hours. Usually from 12-5 am was the so called window of opportunity. The Team had set the entire house up and then decided to take a break. It was time for coffee and a snack. Their would be no more alcohol intake. It was time to get on the investigation and tackle it as the professional's they were.

At about 1 am the shit hit the fan out of nowhere. As the washer and dryer in the basement would both seem to be operating on their own. The thing that was ironic to the team. Was that not a piece of equipment one had been setup down stairs. Tracey knew then this was a bad situation. To have activity happen only where cameras hadn't been placed. That scared Tracey very deeply.

She was in shock at this time. "This thing is very powerful and smart" she said to herself. She had the whole team go down stairs with her as they video taped with a hand held recorder. The washer and dryer as she would turn them both off. And then the team turned towards the basement stairs to head back up. In that moment the lights turned off in an instant. Everyone panicked right then and there.

(Chapter 6)

(The Demon's Domain)

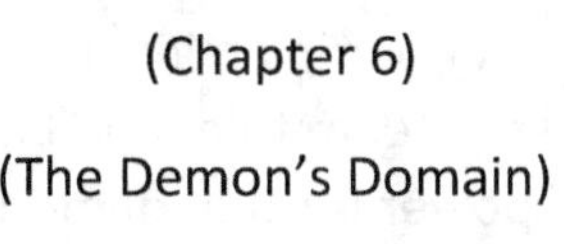

Tracey yelled at the team to be quiet. The crew could only be heard breathing rapidly. As they all stood there in the total black of darkness. Soon after they heard the door knob of the back basement door being fumbled with. As if someone was outside and trying to come in. Then over on the other side of the stairs they could all hear what sounded like hooves walking towards them.

Then out of nowhere as they all stood in total shock. A low blood curdling growl could be heard as something were now clearly standing before them. They could all feel the air from the demons breath being blown upon them all. It was so Traumatizing that they all almost passed out in that moment. The stink of Sulphur now settled in the room. Tracey yelled at the team to grab her shirt. And follow her as she led them up and out of the basement.

As they all finally reached the top of the stairs. Tracey closed the basement door in an instant. Immediately locking it back securing it for the moment. Tracey then told the team to not go back down in the basement for any reason what so ever. That it was now a place of power for that demon alone. They all knew their was now a presence down below them.

In which they were all well passed being freaked out at that point in time. It was now 2 am and the prime time for things to start happening. Sims wanted to go upstairs and check on things. Tracey gave him the OK. As he set out towards the stairs that would lead him to the second floor. As he got to the top of the steps. A baseball rolled right past his feet and into the bedroom on the right side of the staircase.

As the baseball entered the bedroom the door slammed in an instant. And the light bulb above him shattered. The remnants of glass now fell upon the top of his head. As he stood in the dark. As he turned his head to look down at the team just below him. He was immediately sent airborne as he now flew in the air downwards towards the first floor.

Sims screamed ever so loudly as he flew down the stairs missing each step. Finally his body crashing into the wall as he fell unconscious in an instant. The whole team yelled out in fear now in that moment. Unsure of what to do next. They all ran over towards him to check and see if he were still alive. Mike checked his neck for a pulse. Their wasn't any sign of life what so ever in Sims.

(Chapter 7)

(The Demon's Domain)

He was gone, Mike knew for certain his friend was deceased. He looked over to Tracey and lowered his head. Everyone walked over towards the couch and chairs. They all needed a short rest. To come to terms that they had just lost a key member of their team. Their had to be a decision made and soon. Was this even worth going on any further ?

They had already lost one member and were only a couple hours into their investigation. It had been dangerous ever since they'd first walked into the house. So what to do from that moment forward was the question that needed to be answered. First and foremost, before going any further with anything. Treading the waters very lightly would be the mind set if they did decide to go on.

They had just seen their good friend apparently get thrown down the stairs. And killed in less than a fraction of a seconds time. The whole team was now in a state of panic. Not knowing if they should carry on or quit the mission and just go home. Tracey was going to try and push her team to move on forward. She really wanted to help this family. The Roger family that she had come to know and become friends with as well.

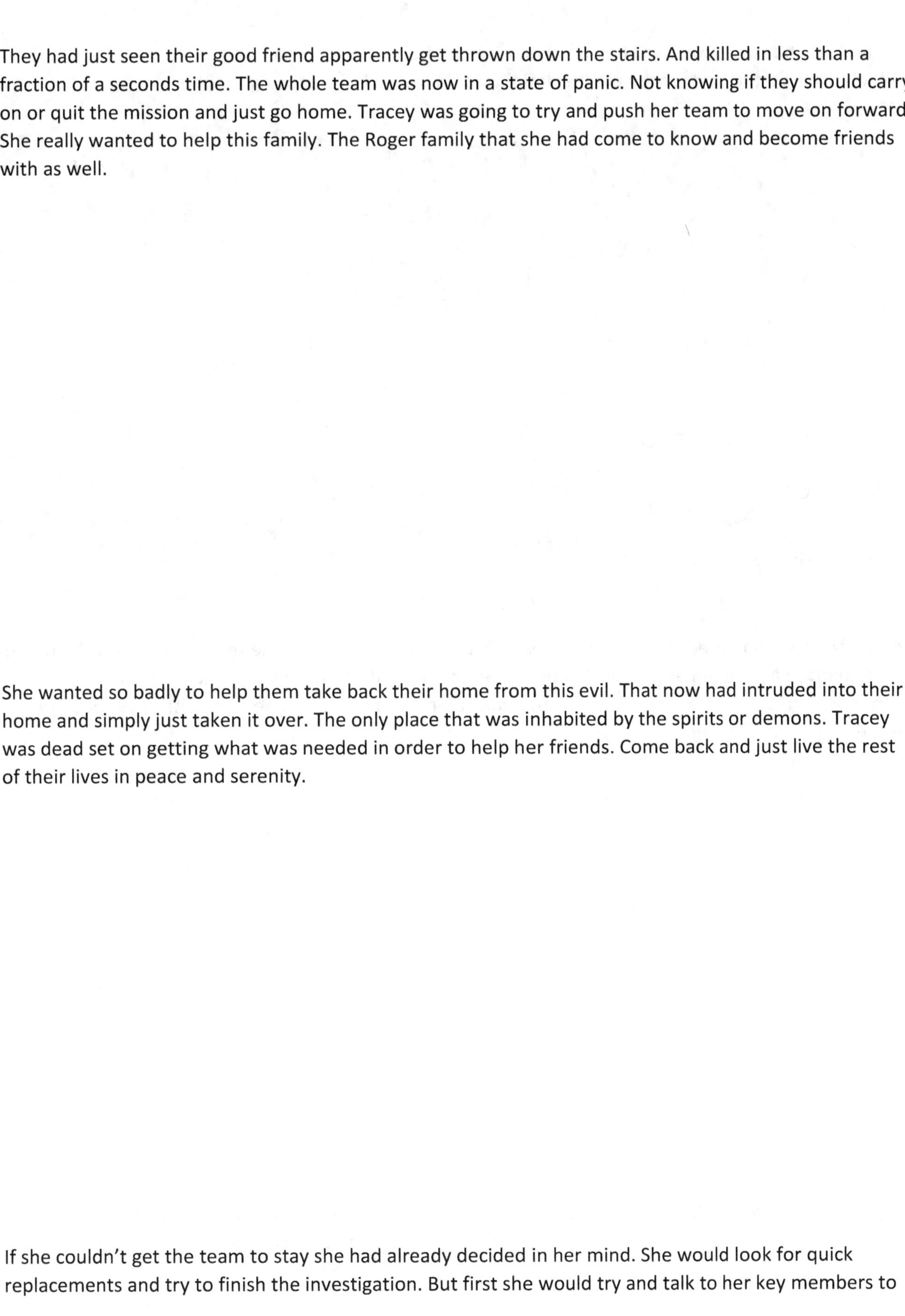

She wanted so badly to help them take back their home from this evil. That now had intruded into their home and simply just taken it over. The only place that was inhabited by the spirits or demons. Tracey was dead set on getting what was needed in order to help her friends. Come back and just live the rest of their lives in peace and serenity.

If she couldn't get the team to stay she had already decided in her mind. She would look for quick replacements and try to finish the investigation. But first she would try and talk to her key members to stay and ride out the storm with her. She would even offer them a bit more money to stay if in fact she had to. It was that important to her. She definetly didn't want to lose the fight either.

(Chapter 8)

(The Demon's Domain)

So as they all sat and tried to catch their breath. Tracey calmly discussed the team's options. Whether to stay And make a huge impact possibly in their field of research. Or they could tuck their tails in and run. Even though this situation was far more dangerous than another predicament they had ever been in before as a team or a unit.

In that moment the two brothers and Tracey were in fact the only three members of the team left. The brothers immediately responded at the exact same time. Agreeing to stay with their boss lady. For the long-term. To try and get the evidence needed in order to find out just exactly what type of haunting this was. Tracey automatically said she was having a priest come out to the property.

But she also stated that this could be a huge problem. The problem was that they were way out in Gettysburg Pennsylvania. Quite a distance away from any church. The farm was located in Adam's County. Which in fact was about a forty five minute drive to the nearest town. The trip would have to be made immediately. So the team all locked the house up and left for town.

Upon their arrival they would have three churches in all to choose from. The Gettysburg Four Square Church, The Gettysburg United Methodist Church Of God. Or last but not least, the Gettysburg Presbyterian Church. The team would debate on exactly which Church to choose from the three choices. Atleast they had three chances of getting help by a pastor.

The key would be to have faith in which ever if any decided to assist them. And also hope the pastor would have immense faith in God himself. They needed a good strong man of Faith if they had any chance of success. The house was definetly haunted. And by far the worst house they'd ever worked in. Tracey got out of the car and walked up to the front door of the Church itself.

(Chapter 9)

(The Demon's Domain)

Upon knocking she pulled the door and it opened right up. The door hadn't even been locked. That was wild to Tracey. She hadn't experienced that since the 1980's when her parents and friends in her home town slept in their homes with the doors unlocked. This town must have had trust in its own people to a certain extent.

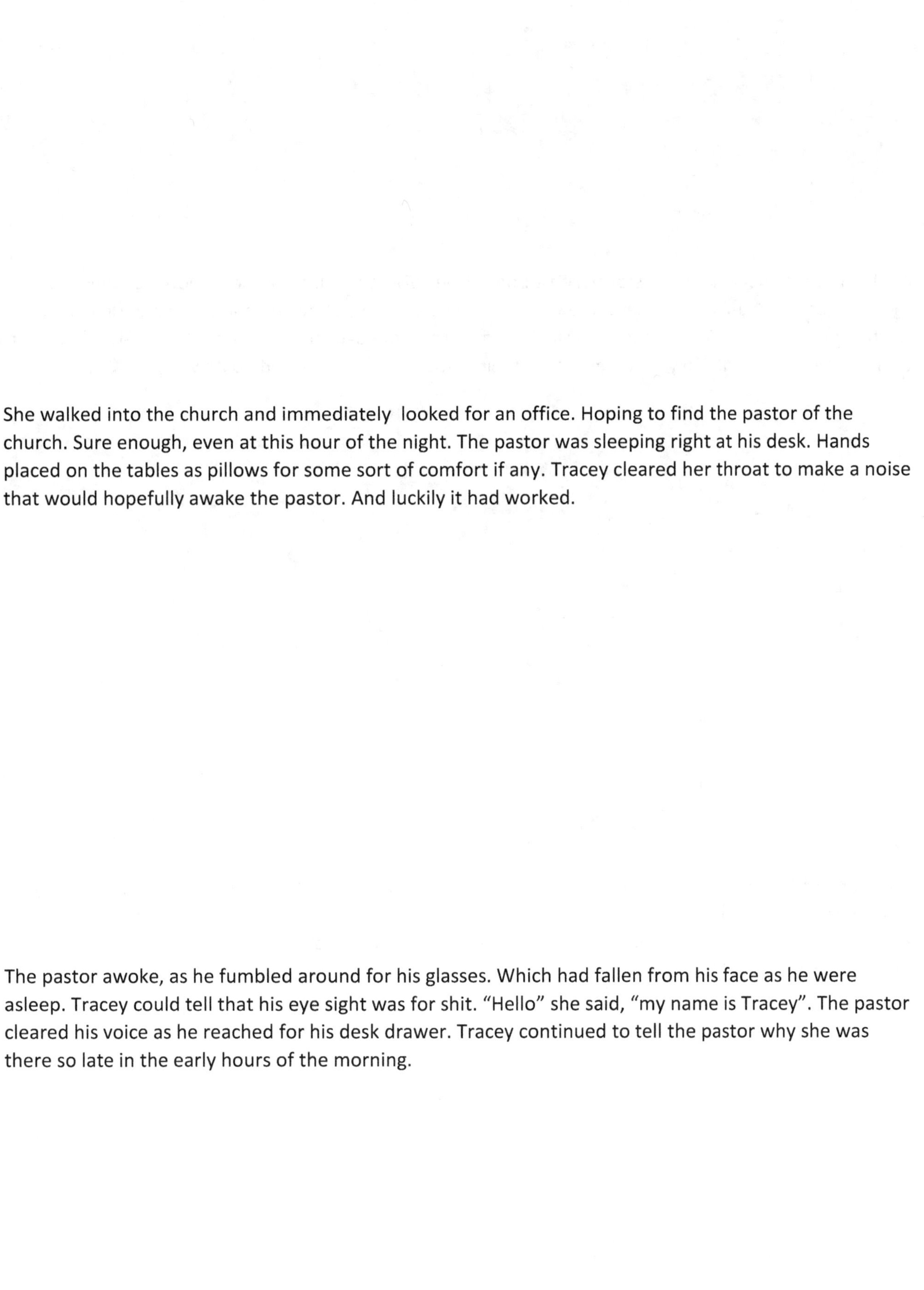

She walked into the church and immediately looked for an office. Hoping to find the pastor of the church. Sure enough, even at this hour of the night. The pastor was sleeping right at his desk. Hands placed on the tables as pillows for some sort of comfort if any. Tracey cleared her throat to make a noise that would hopefully awake the pastor. And luckily it had worked.

The pastor awoke, as he fumbled around for his glasses. Which had fallen from his face as he were asleep. Tracey could tell that his eye sight was for shit. "Hello" she said, "my name is Tracey". The pastor cleared his voice as he reached for his desk drawer. Tracey continued to tell the pastor why she was there so late in the early hours of the morning.

As she finished speaking the pastor pulled a bottle from within the drawer itself a bottle of Whiskey. He then replied back to Tracey. "I have known you were here". "I watched you and your team drive into town earlier" he said. "The Roger family left out of here weeks ago" he again stated as he switched over to the subject at hand. "So you're here to rid their home of evil" ? he asked politely.

"Well first off", "we have to call the Sheriff's office. And get them to follow us back out there.". "They will have to investigate the scene", the pastor said. "Just to make sure a crime hasn't been committed". "Well I'm hoping we have something documented off of our cameras" Tracey replied back. "We have them setup all around the house".

(Chapter 10)

(The Demons Domain)

"By the way", "I am Pastor Price", "It is very nice to meet you Tracey". As he replied back to her once again. "I only hope you do have something on video showing some form of activity". "Or you and your whole team will be looked at immensely". "Pertaining to the death of Sims". "And what it was that actually took place just before his passing".

"None of that matters now" Tracey replied back in an instant. "He is gone" she said sadly. "I know what happened", "But it can't be explained" she stated. Tracey stood there for a few minutes. With eyes that looked as if she had traveled off to a far distance. As she seemed to be day dreaming in those few short moments. Just as she'd done after the death of one of her great friends.

Pastor Price snapped his fingers softly. Tracey. Asking her the question he was now seeking from her. "So it looked as if he were pushed down the stairs" ? he asked kindly. "Yes" Tracey replied immediately in a split second. "But so strongly that he never hit a single step on the way down". "That was the most frightening part of it all". She stated as she started to tremble.

Pastor Price picked up on her shaking quickly. "Well I believe you Tracey", he said softly. "And I'm sorry for your deep loss". "Now let's call the Sheriff". "We need an authority figure there with us". He said strongly. "We not only need him for protection but". "He has to see this for himself". "OK" Tracey replied back. "Let's do this" she said. The pastor called the Sheriff's office.

The phone was answered quickly. "Sheriff's office", this is Sheriff Landers speaking". The pastor explained the current situation to the Sheriff and then hung up the phone. "He is on his way" the pastor said to Tracey. "He's only five minutes away from us" Pastor Price stated. "So let's hit the road". Tracey then stopped him in his tracks as she placed her arm on his left shoulder.

(Chapter 11)

(The Demon's Domain)

"I have to ask you" Tracey said to the pastor. "Do you think that a Bible will help us" ? "Or maybe even some Holy Water" ? The pastor said back to Tracey in an instant. "You may be right" he said back to her. "Better to be safe than sorry". He then walked back to the corner of his office and grabbed a bottle from the cabinet drawer. "Come on" he said to her. "The Sheriff will be here any minute now".

The two new friends walked towards the front doors of the church. As they exited the Sheriff pulled up next to their vehicle. As he got out of his car he said to Tracey. "Hello I am Sheriff Landers". "And you must be Tracey" he again said. "Nice to meet you too" Tracey replied back to the Sheriff. "Well Come on let's go shouted the pastor". "It's apparent we've got bigger fish to fry" he stated.

They all got into separate vehicles and set out. Heading back to the Roger farm. Their would be a forty five minute window before they would arrive. Tracey was hoping that within the past Ninety or so minutes. That some sort of activity had been captured on the cameras. That would without a doubt show the Sheriff as well as Pastor Price. Exactly what had been going on there.

Forty five minutes later after a long and drawn out drive. With not many words being said. They arrived back at the farm. Jumping out of the cars as they all headed in towards the house. As they all got up on the front porch. The Sheriff had noticed that the front door was already open. He was shocked by that. "Did you leave the door open when you left he asked"

"No" Tracey replied. "That's what I am saying" she said intensely. They all headed into the house slowly. As they hit the living room the Sheriff could see Sims over by the wall. Blood had been splattered back behind his head. As if his head had been banged up against it repeatedly. Tracey immediately noticed a book that was over off to the right side of the room sitting on the floor.

(Chapter 12)

(The Demon's Domain)

Tracey stuck her arm out as she pointed her finger towards the book that was sitting on the floor. She immediately said out loud. "Look" "that wasn't there when we left the house". "Now it's on the floor, "that doesn't make any sense at all to me. She then walked over to the camera that was facing the book shelf and removed it from the tri-pod.

Tracey reminded the camera back to the moment they left and had shut the front door. She told everyone to come and look at what had happened. As soon as they had shut the front door. The book had flown out and off of the bookshelf. "What caused this book to fly off of the bookshelf" ? she now asked the Sheriff. As he was locked in on the camera itself.

"What in the hell did that" ? He asked outlook. Hoping to get an answer from someone in the room. "That was a damn Ghost" Arron shouted out nervously. "They've taken over this house" he again shouted loudly. As if he were growing aggravated with the mission. He then walked out of the room and into the kitchen.

"This is crazy" said the Sheriff. "What can we do" he asked Pastor Price as he now grew nervous as well. The pastor told everyone to calm down. That it wasn't wise to lose your cool he told the entire group. "If we become weak they can over take our body" he stated to everyone. The Sheriff now walked over and checked Sims. As he looked up the stairs.

In that moment they all heard a door open upstairs. Then shortly after that the pounding of hooves could be heard walking through the upstairs hallway. The Sheriff stood there in fear now in that moment. As his whole body tightened up like a rock. Then the baseball could be seen slowly rolling through the hallway as it stopped at the foot of the stairs.

(Chapter 13)

(The Demon's Domain)

The next few moments were so frightening as the ball just layed there. Then as they all stopped to stare at it. It came flying down the stairs. At a very fast speed. The Sheriff ducking as everyone else did. As the baseball crashed into the wall. Just above Sims deceased body. Making a huge hole in the wall as it went completely through and now had fallen down in behind the drywall.

"Ok" said the Sheriff. "What should we do" ?as he now trembled in total fear. "Everyone sit down" the pastor yelled out everyone. "I have to Bless this house somehow". "Without dying in the process". "This house has been totally consumed by an evil entity of some form" he stated. "I need to go to each room and sprinkle the Holy water". "And cast this evil from this home".

Tracey agreed with the pastor on the idea. A plan was put forth within the next few minutes. The group would follow closely behind the pastor as he worked with the Holy water in each room. Even the Sheriff was with them. He was already present and had seen first hand the power of this entity. He was without a doubt scared to death.

They walked into the kitchen first and would work their way back to the living room and then head up the stairs toward the other two rooms. Hitting the attic last but not least. All four of the group members now stuck together tightly in fear. Tracey told them to shake it. But that alone wasn't going to be the instant cure that they were all now hoping for.

As the group entered the kitchen all was well until Price opened up the Holy water. In that moment the kitchen door would open as a huge burst of wind now flew inside. Leaves and twigs now flew about in the air. It blocked everyone's eye sight at that time. The pastor knew now evil was present. He started to sprinkle the water as he quoted from the Bible.

(Chapter 14)

(The Demon's Domain)

As soon as he had opened that Bible it started. He'll and chaos now had taken over. The Sheriff fought through the oncoming winds and Debris and steadily walked towards the kitchen door. Finally closing It as he secured it shut. As the door had been closed the kitchen lights shattered out of nowhere. Glass from the eight bulbs that were lined with a glass cover fell allover everyone.

Everyone immediately ran into the dining room. Outside the storm was brewing heavily. Lightning was now flashing around the whole entire house. The rain could be heard in that moment hitting the roof. It was then they'd heard the hooves walking about on the second floor once again. It brought great fear to the whole group.

The foot steps were now growing louder with time. It seemed as if whatever this thing was it was becoming stronger with each incident that occurred. Something had to be done and now. Pastor Price told everyone that they had to push forward. That the house had to be cleansed before the spirits became to strong and couldn't be cast out.

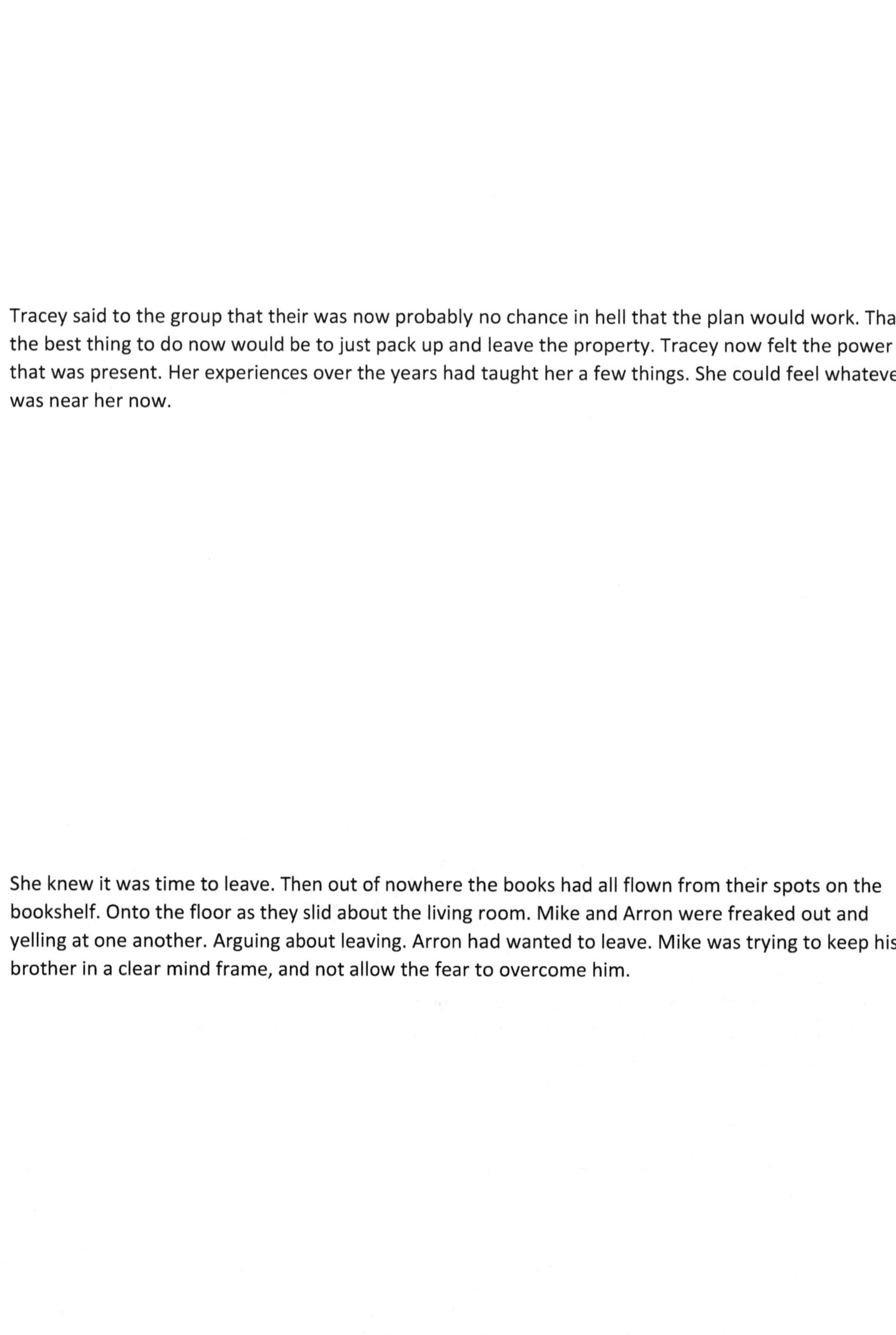

Tracey said to the group that their was now probably no chance in hell that the plan would work. That the best thing to do now would be to just pack up and leave the property. Tracey now felt the power that was present. Her experiences over the years had taught her a few things. She could feel whatever was near her now.

She knew it was time to leave. Then out of nowhere the books had all flown from their spots on the bookshelf. Onto the floor as they slid about the living room. Mike and Arron were freaked out and yelling at one another. Arguing about leaving. Arron had wanted to leave. Mike was trying to keep his brother in a clear mind frame, and not allow the fear to overcome him.

(Chapter 15)

(The Demon's Domain)

The Sheriff told everyone to relax as he pulled his gun. In an attempt to go up the stairs and onto the second floor. The pastor told him that the gun wouldn't help at all. And in fact that he would probably upset the entities even more by doing so. But the Sheriff didn't listen to him at all as he now walked up the steps as fast as he could.

When he arrived at the top of the stairs. He looked left and then to the right as fast as he could while in total fear. Tracey yelled up to the Sheriff, telling him to relax and put the gun away. Pastor Price walked up the stairs as well. As fast as he could possibly do so. Holding the bottle of Holy water in his hands. They both went into the first bedroom. The pastor started to pull quotes from the Bible.

Then the two finished the first bedroom. They turned around and headed towards the second bedroom. As he started quoting from the Bible once again. As they entered the bedroom. The two of them looked around as if they too felt something present in the room. In that moment just two steps of the hooves were heard. Then a deep low growl that seemed to be that of the Devil himself.

The Sheriff and the Pastor both froze stiff. Neither of them could move a muscle in their bodies. Tracey yelled up to the two new teammates. To see if they were both OK, she could no longer see them. Their was no reply at all. In that moment she ran up the stairs as fast as she could, to see if the two were still alive.

When she got up to the top of the stairs. Tracey turned immediately to the right and ran towards the second bedroom. Upon walking in she seen the both of them. Sticking against the wall in two separate sections of the room itself. Both men acted as if they couldn't breath. Tracey then looked about the room.

(Chapter 16)

(The Demon's Domain)

Every cross in the room that was hanging from the walls. Was turned upside down as if they were some sort of insult. The pastor and the Sheriff now screamed out in sheer agony. Their finger nails were being ripped out one by one. At the same exact time this was happening. But nobody was present in the room. How could this be possible Tracey thought to herself.

She had lost all hope at this point in time. It all had been undone by something so powerful. The Holy water had seemed to only aggravate whatever it was that was dwelling in the home now. Tracey now felt totally defeated. She stood there in that moment taking it all in. She then yelled down stairs to Mike and Arron. To bring up the tri-pods and cameras quickly.

The brothers were hesitant at first. But then managed to muster enough courage to do what their boss had asked of them. They ran up the stairs as quickly as possible with the cameras. Tracey then told them to place a tri-pod and camera in each doorway. As soon as Mike and Arron had done what she had asked. The Sheriff and the Pastor fell to the floor in an instant.

Everyone now took a deep breath as the two injured men now got up off of the floor and onto their feet once again. The Sheriff and Pastor Price were both bleeding. Each of them dripping blood from out of their fingertips. It looked quite painful in fact. Tracey now ordered everyone back down stairs. The group all rushed as fast as possible to get down all of the steps.

As they all grabbed a seat Tracey went to the kitchen to grab something. If anything could be found. That the two injured teammates could possibly use to wrap their injuries up for atleast the time being. Nothing could be found but a kitchen apron. It was the only thing Tracey could find. She grabbed a knife from one of the kitchen drawers.

She started to cut the apron up with the knife as fast as she could. Trying to make a couple of wraps for the Pastor as well as the Sheriff. They had came out to help with the situation. Only to get hurt badly in the process. And Tracey had now in that moment. Felt horrible about even involving the two in this hellacious escapade. From the start shed had a horrible feeling about this mission.

(Chapter 17)

(The Demon's Domain)

She then carried cut strips of apron into the living room. Handing sections of the cut cloth to each of the injured men. At this time not a noise could be heard from upstairs any longer. It seemed to of died down atleast for the moment. The team now sat and discussed what if anything else could be done to rid the house of its evil.

The Sheriff calmly interrupted Tracey with a rude awakening. "Sorry girl", he said to her calmly. "It is time that we all most definetly leave this house" he said in a firm voice. "There is nothing left that can be done here". He again said as he finished giving the final answer. "Agreed" replied Tracey as she put her head down in defeat. Letting out a huge exhale of breath in that moment.

Mike and Arron started to pack up the equipment as they too had started to feel defeat for the first time in the air. Tracey sat there for a minute. As she thought over the process of the investigation. From top to bottom she thought about the whole night. The only answer she had learned from this ordeal. Was that when the cameras had been put in place during an attack they had suddenly stopped.

Tracey couldn't quite put together why that attack had stopped when the cameras were placed in each of the bedrooms. She scrambled hard through her brain. Trying to come up with something, if any one thing that may work. She couldn't come up with an answer. Then it hit her like a ton of bricks. The entities had stopped and tried to gather power from the devices themselves.

Or the evil spirits had stopped in that moment. Because they didn't want to be captured on film doing anything evil. Or they were flat out intrigued by the cameras that were giving them attention. The process was crazy she thought. But it would be the only conclusions that made any sense at all. Tracey then asked the Pastor for his opinion on the matter.

(Chapter 18)

(The Demon's Domain)

As soon as Pastor Price had heard the question from Tracey an answer was immediately given back in return. It was a huge flat No. "We have to go and now" was the answer that had been given back to her. The Pastor even knew that this was in fact way above his pay grade. He had done all he could to rid the house of the evil that now lurked inside.

The team was still packing up all of the equipment. When downstairs the sound of hooves could be heard walking around. Then   all of a sudden they could be heard coming up the stairs and that freaked everyone out. Mike and Arron were now hurrying a fast as they could. Just off in the hallway the sounds could be heard even louder as the demon was getting closer to the top of the basement stairs.

Then the sounds stopped. There was a sudden silence that spooked everyone. Then soft knocks could be heard at the basement door. Knocks that sounded as if they were coming from a child. But as no one answered the sounds had become louder and louder over a period of thirty seconds time. Now the knocks were so loud. It sounded like pure power behind them.

At times the group felt like the wooden door would just shatter into a million pieces. Tracey was now scared to death. She said "The hell with it. "Let's just get out here people". "This is beyond crazy". "This whole investigation has been nothing more than a pain in my ass". Tracey shouted out very loudly in madness at this point. She was at the point of becoming hysterical.

As soon as Tracey stopped shooting video. A few minutes had went by. The knocking had finally stopped. It would come in patterns of 30 second intervals as it would slow and then suddenly stop. As the sounds stopped this time a window broke out in the kitchen. Making it seem that someone was trying to get in from the back door of the kitchen.

(Chapter 19)

(The Demon's Domain)

Then out of nowhere every window in the house shattered all at once. The wind from the storm outside now ripped the Glass all around the area of the first floor of the home The tiny pieces of glass hit the team in the face as they shut their eyes to keep from being blinded. The rain was now whipping about also. Mixed in with leaves and dirt as well.

It had made a huge mess of the living room. Tracey told her friends that the equipment were to be left upstairs. That it wasn't important enough to risk a life. She wanted the rest of her people out of the house and in one piece. That was all Tracey was worried about at this point. She told the group of men to get ready as soon as possible. That it was time to go.

They all just dropped the bags and cases of equipment on the living room floor. As they did the group headed towards the front door. The Sheriff tried to open the door as he turned the knob. But it wouldn't open. Pastor Price told the team that the only way out was to dive out of the front windows. Tracey ran over to the windows to make sure the glass was out of the frames.

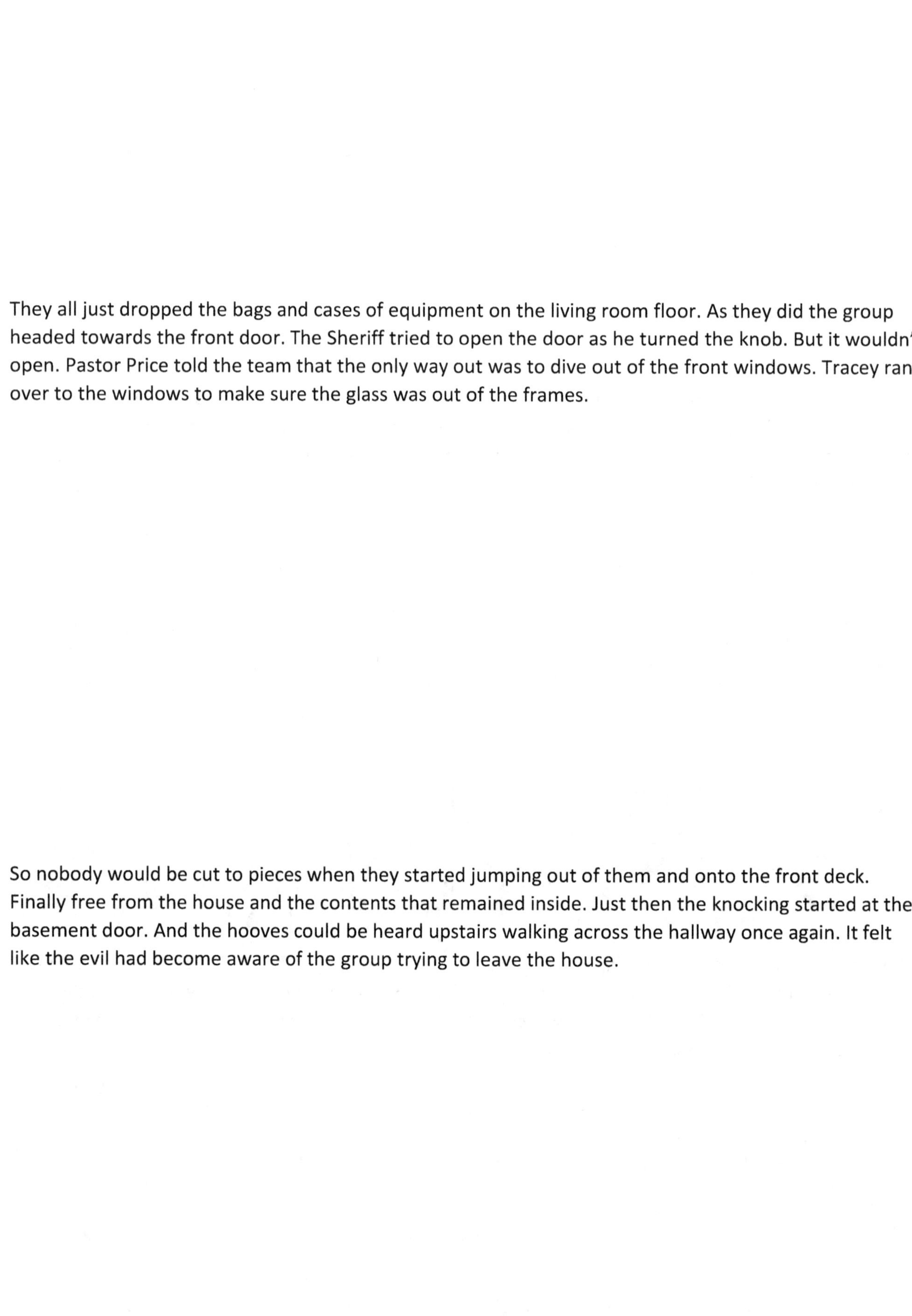

So nobody would be cut to pieces when they started jumping out of them and onto the front deck. Finally free from the house and the contents that remained inside. Just then the knocking started at the basement door. And the hooves could be heard upstairs walking across the hallway once again. It felt like the evil had become aware of the group trying to leave the house.

The Sheriff couldn't believe what was happening. He had thought it was all bullshit. But knew now for certain the family had been telling him the truth all along. And that he had enabled these evil spirits to become so strong over time. By not helping the Roger family in their time of need. Never fully investigating their cry for help. Now It was well passed the point of no return.

(Chapter 20)

(The Demon's Domain)

The crazy thing about the whole mission was the fact that the team never made it passed the first floor really. The attic had still been untouched during the investigation. The living room and the kitchen had cameras set up. That was all the team had managed to do. Tracey told the Sheriff to go first. To get out of the house. Before anyone else got attacked and killed.

The Sheriff took a couple of steps back as he zoned in on the jump he was about to make. Out and onto the from deck. He ran quickly and dove towards the opening of the window. His body guided perfectly through. Shortly after the jump he hit the front deck and rolled smashing into the wooden posts that held the entire railing and the whole porch together as well.

Tracey then told the Pastor to go and go quickly. That it was far to dangerous to go any further with the blessing of the house. Pastor Price was so upset with the fact that he couldn't help the Rogers family get rid of this evil. That was now ruling the home as it slowly consumed the house. The pastor handed Tracey the bottle of blessed water.

As he handed Tracey the bottle. Pastor Price took off and quickly dove in the air. As he hit the front deck he slid a bit further. Hitting the rails and breaking the posts as he fell over and off the side of the porch itself. Landing in a huge pond of water and mud. It had formed shortly after an intense lightning strike. That much was known for the pond hadn't been there upon the teams arrival earlier in the day.

Now there were only the two brothers Mike and Arron and Tracey left. Tracey told Arron to go next. Arron ran immediately and jumped through the window. As he hit the front porch the Sheriff stopped him from sliding off and down into the huge puddle as the Pastor had just done moments before. The Sheriff had grabbed him just in time.

Mike went next as he listened to Tracey. After all, she was the boss. Mike ran as fast as he could. He wanted out of this house very badly. As he dove through the front window. The Basement door had suddenly shattered into splinters. And the sound of hooves could be heard once again. Tracey turned to look into the kitchen as Mike had made it through the window.

(Chapter 21)

(The Demon's Domain)

Tracey was now in shock as she stood frozen in fear. Whatever had been held behind the basement door was now present. And it was Somewhere in the kitchen or the dining room. Remnants of the basement door now laid allover the floor of the kitchen. Tracey was now scrambling through her brain. On what she would do next.

Something was pulling her to go back up the stairs. She thought quickly on what she should do. Jump out of the window ? or go back up stairs and grab both of the cameras. They were both still in action as they sat on tri-pods. And with no doubt were still recording footage. And had been for about thirty minutes now at the very least. She decided to try and grab at the very least one of the two.

Tracey decided to go for it all as she jolted off and up the stairs. As she hit the top of the landing and now found herself running for the back bedroom. What she seen next blew her away. The wooden Crosses on each side of the room that had been nailed to the wall. For prayer and decoration as well. Were now spinning round and round swiftly while they stayed in place on the wall.

The drawers to the dressers had all been pulled out and their contents were now laying all around the room on the floor. Tracey reached to grab the camera from off of the tri-pod. As she did her hand was smacked down in a flash. She was now frightened to death. She stood their, frozen in fear. As she felt the rush go through her body.

She knew she had to grab the camera. At all costs she had to manage someway. To get possession of the device and bolt for the stairs. She now thought to herself. I will grab it fast as I possibly can and run. She reached out again as quick as she could. Only to get smacked across her face. Knocking her to her knees. Tracey let out a rage full and very loud scream.

(Chapter 22)

(The Demon's Domain)

Tracey got up to her feet and instantly dove for the camera. As she went passed the Tri-pod she had managed to grab the camera finally as she then hit the floor as she slid into the wall. Knocking one of the Crosses off of its nail as it now fell on her leg in an upside down formation. She looked down to see the cross. As she now attempted to grab it with her right hand.

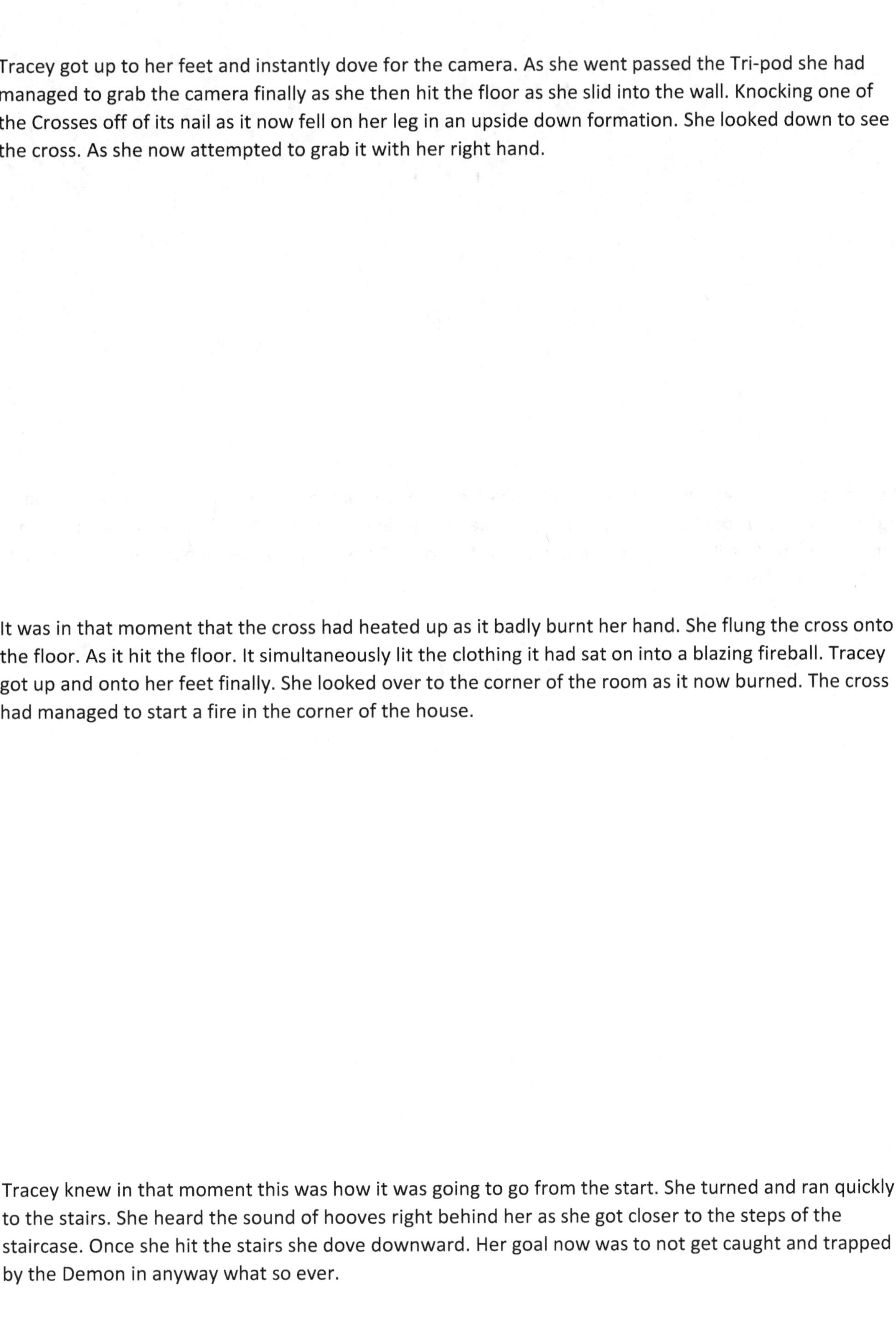

It was in that moment that the cross had heated up as it badly burnt her hand. She flung the cross onto the floor. As it hit the floor. It simultaneously lit the clothing it had sat on into a blazing fireball. Tracey got up and onto her feet finally. She looked over to the corner of the room as it now burned. The cross had managed to start a fire in the corner of the house.

Tracey knew in that moment this was how it was going to go from the start. She turned and ran quickly to the stairs. She heard the sound of hooves right behind her as she got closer to the steps of the staircase. Once she hit the stairs she dove downward. Her goal now was to not get caught and trapped by the Demon in anyway what so ever.

She hit and slid on her butt as she quickly tumbled down the stairs that led to the first floor. As she hit the bottom step Tracey ran in an instant and made her last and final dive. Out of the window and onto front porch. The Sheriff had reached out in the last second. Grabbing her as he stopped her from rolling off of the front porch.

Finally they had all made it out. With the exception of Sims. He was still lying at the wall at the edge of the last step to the upstairs. They had all forgotten the poor man as they all fled for their own lives. Now to go in and get him or not remained the question that needed to be answered. And it had to be decided fast.

(Chapter 23)

(The Demon's Domain)

The house was on fire as the second floor was now burning very intensely. The smoke now pouring. The Sheriff blurted out to Tracey. "Should we go in and get him or no" ? The Sheriff asked. He then waited for an answer. In the meantime he was now on the radio calling in the fire department. And calling in backup also to put the fire out.

As the Sheriff stepped out of his car. The second floor windows blew outward. Shattering from the intense heat. Flames came out of the back window and took form of the Demon inside. It's horned head shaped perfectly in form. The whole team looked upward to see it. Suddenly behind them they all heard the Horses scream. As the roof of the barn was now on fire.

"The Horses, "we have to get them put of there" yelled Tracey. The whole team had forgotten about Sims in that moment. They all now ran towards the barn. In an effort to release the horses. That were in a great deal of distress. Only the top of the roof was on fire. If the team hurried up. They just might be able to get them out of there in time.

The rain still poured down in a fury. The group all arrived at the barn. Running in immediately as they opened the gates of each stall. The horses ran out of the barn and into the safety of the field. Everyone ran towards the main door. To get back out of the barn. The roof suddenly collapsed and fell onto the ground. As it had fallen it had trapped the last horse. Killing it instantly.

Tracey now found herself pointing her finger to each of the group. She was counting heads and realized their was one member missing. "We are missing one person" said Tracey. "The Pastor is missing" she said as she ran back to the side door of the barn. As she opened the door flames poured out towards the door. Tracey ducked down out of pure instinct in that moment.

(Chapter 24)

(The Demon's Domain)

Just barely, she had managed to duck under the flames as they blew passed her head. As she shut the side door to the barn stables back shut. The Pastor had not made it back out in time. The roof had fallen on top of him taking his life and a horse as well. Tracey once again felt pure defeat in that moment. She slid down the fence of the field post onto her butt. As she once again took a much needed deep breath.

She was now soaked to the gill with rain water that had her clothes totally drenched. She took a deep breath and let it out. She now stared at the barn. It was fully engulfed in flames. The Sheriff came over to her and kneeled downward. "Tracey" he said to her in a lone tone of voice. "You did the best you could". "And that is all you can do". "I failed in each and every way" she replied back to Sheriff Landers.

"Nobody could have won this battle" Sheriff Landers said to Tracey "Nobody". Their were Four of them left standing. The sounds of the Fire engines and the Police cars could now be heard. Just off in the distance coming their way. Minutes later they'd all arrived. The fire hoses were being pulled from the trucks as the firemen got ready to battle the house and barn fire.

Tracey stood up and realized that they had forgotten about Sims. Who was inside still and being burnt up possibly. Their was nothing they could do now. The firemen weren't going to allow anyone inside the house. And that was a fact. Mike and Arron were banged up a little bit. But were both alive and well. That was all that mattered as of now. Two had been lossed and Tracey was just glad she hadn't lossed everyone.

She knew whatever had taken over and had placed terror over the home. Was a very powerful demon. It had never even showed itself. Not one damn time. But it never really had to either. It was scary enough just as it was. To spread fear And to make others flee from the home. The Firemen had now put the fire out throughout the entire house. The house had been saved luckily.

(Chapter 25)

(The Demon's Domain)

Which in fact they should have let the house burn down to the ground in all honesty. The town would have been a much safer place to live. That was a known fact as of now. The team would be able to stay and watch the property for a while. It wouldn't be safe until this house was properly blessed or tore to the ground whichever came first. Were Tracey's thoughts on the matter.

The towns only ambulance arrived an hour later. And the firemen went in and pulled Sim's body out of the God forsaken home. It had been as of now in that moment. Thee most haunted and evil place that Tracey and the team had ever investigated before. Nothing came close to the Gettysburg Farm. Not by a long shot that was for certain.

The fire was still burning at the barn. The whole thing had completely burned up within A matter of thirty minutes. The wood was so old and dry rotted. It had burned up like a wheat field in the dog days of July. The heat from both fires had heated up the whole area if only for a few minutes. The rain was finally starting to slow down at the time.

The firemen and the Ambulance driver had asked the Sheriff why were all of these people out at the Rogers Farm while they were gone ? He told them why. And soon after that they had packed up and left as fast as they possibly could. Now the group were left to deal with the madness all alone again with pure evil lurking just inside the home.

Tracey begged the Sheriff to just burn what was left of the Roger house down. As she pleaded to him it could be built allover again. But the law was the law and Sheriff Landers had to uphold it. At any cost, that had to be the way. So in that moment Tracey had to take it all in and accept it. The battle the loss of life the defeat all of it.

She had never been in a situation like this one. Two men had been killed while trying to save the livelihood of others. But this evil was that of another caliber. And it had grown to be so strong over time. Tracey surely thought that it had been the Devil himself that they'd encountered and had battled with. She had sensed his presence from the start.

(Chapter 26)

(The Demon's Domain)

She gathered the group together, as they all sat down in the field. In between what was now known as two haunted buildings. Tracey restarted the camera that had been up in the second floor bedroom for thirty minute's. It was where the most power had shown itself. They watched as the camera had recorded what seemed to be an outline of a horned creature with a muscular upper body.

The second half of the creatures body was even more frightening. This thing had legs of a horse and the hooves of a goat. Surely the Devil. Or a close resemblance to him at the very least. It had shown the drawers being flung open while nobody at all were present. It also revealed the clothes being flung out of the drawers piece by piece. By some form of entity. That were present at the time.

And last but not least, the camera had shown just exactly when Tracey had entered the room. Only to be attacked in those few short but very traumatic moments. It had recorded the moment when the Crosses had started to spin on their own while on the wall. And even the moment when Tracey was smacked down and also when she was burned. As well as the fire. When it had first started, and the exact place it had sparked.

So even in defeat and great loss. Their was a victory of some sorts that had been achieved. Maybe just maybe this video could help others after it had been looked at by the Church. Once Tracey had sent copies of it to them all. She was in better spirits now. Knowing that the mission wasn't a total loss. Even though she had bad news for the Rogers family. But good news as well would come from this investigation.

Even though good had come from that situation. Tracey figured that in knowing now what had taken over their farm. They could demolish and re build. That was what she would tell them. It would be the best route for the Roger family. In order to keep them all safe and out of harms way. The team packed up the equipment and secured it in their trunks of the vehicles.

(Chapter 27)

(The Demon's Domain)

The team would start to make their drive home. As they pulled away and drive off of the land and back towards town. Another storm seemed to be moving in on the horizon. This one looked intense as lightning was flashing every few seconds. Followed by huge rumbles of thunder. Tracey was so tired as she would make a four hour drive back home.

She would stop by the Sheriff's office before leaving Gettysburg. To say thank you one last time and also say goodbye to Sheriff Landers. As he were a big help to her during her very short investigation. This one even though it had been cut short. The cameras had still managed to get a lot of great evidence and video also of the Demons actions.

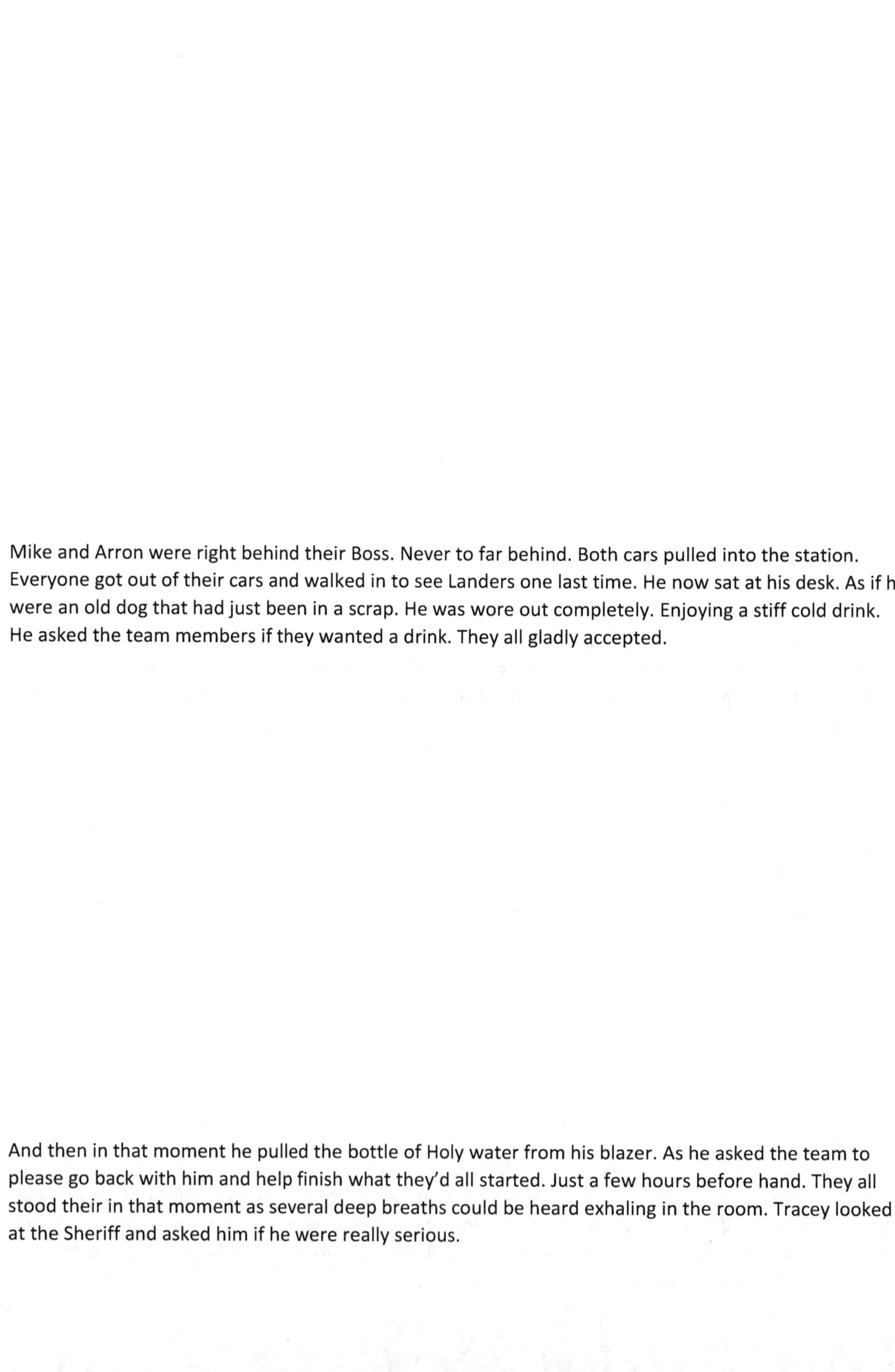

Mike and Arron were right behind their Boss. Never to far behind. Both cars pulled into the station. Everyone got out of their cars and walked in to see Landers one last time. He now sat at his desk. As if he were an old dog that had just been in a scrap. He was wore out completely. Enjoying a stiff cold drink. He asked the team members if they wanted a drink. They all gladly accepted.

And then in that moment he pulled the bottle of Holy water from his blazer. As he asked the team to please go back with him and help finish what they'd all started. Just a few hours before hand. They all stood their in that moment as several deep breaths could be heard exhaling in the room. Tracey looked at the Sheriff and asked him if he were really serious.

And to remember how they had just had their asses handed to them. While trying to rid the Rogers Farm from pure evil. The Sheriff agreed but also had something to say back after Tracey had responded to him. He said to the team in that moment. "We did manage to weaken this evil" he said. "Even if only a little bit". That that could help them get the upper hand if they used the Holy water one more time.

The key would be to rush through the whole house. As they stayed in a tight group. While pouring the Holy water in each room. That was all the Sheriff wanted from the team. He then begged them to help him. Telling them the Rogers family was like family to him. And that he'd grown so close to them all over the years. Tracey sat down and made a stiff drink and thought about it for a few minutes.

(Chapter 28)

(The Demon's Domain)

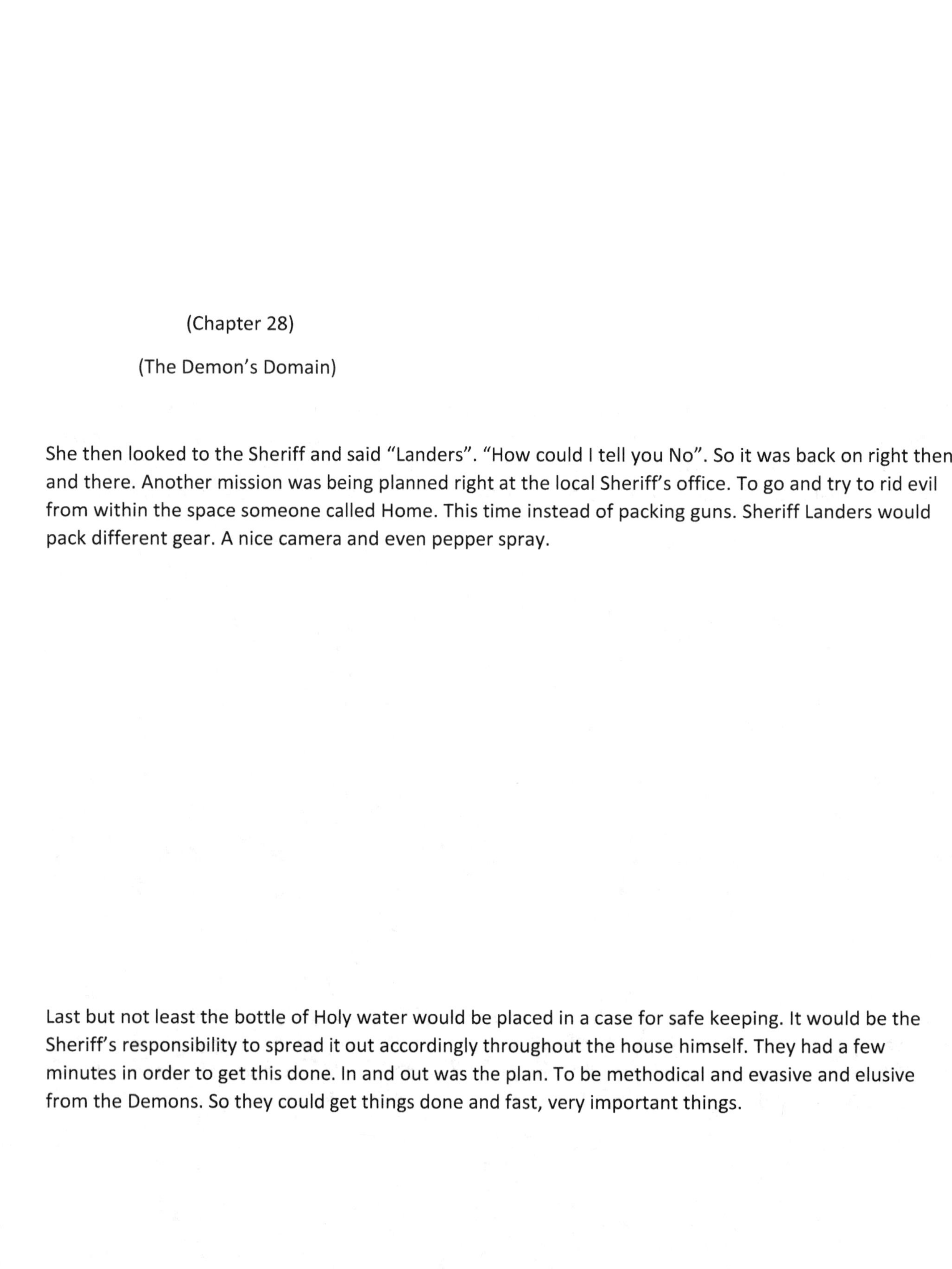

She then looked to the Sheriff and said "Landers". "How could I tell you No". So it was back on right then and there. Another mission was being planned right at the local Sheriff's office. To go and try to rid evil from within the space someone called Home. This time instead of packing guns. Sheriff Landers would pack different gear. A nice camera and even pepper spray.

Last but not least the bottle of Holy water would be placed in a case for safe keeping. It would be the Sheriff's responsibility to spread it out accordingly throughout the house himself. They had a few minutes in order to get this done. In and out was the plan. To be methodical and evasive and elusive from the Demons. So they could get things done and fast, very important things.

To take someone's home back from The Devil or one of his Spawns. Once and for all. The team members were all prepared. As they each had a whole new attitude. They were refreshed again. Finally a feeling of self confidence seemed to be growing amongst them. That was very important in order for a successful mission to be possible.

The team now packed up the new gear. As they all jumped in to their cars. They were going back for round two. They had got their asses handed to them in round one. But now they had a new attitude they were all carrying. And not fear like the first trip in. If success were possible at all, then this would be the time for it to happen.

They all jumped in and started the cars and were off. Back towards the Rogers Farm land. For round two of their fight with a Demon. Possibly even Satan himself. Even though this thing hadn't shown itself fully. Their was a feeling that this was who they'd all encountered while inside that home. And now they wanted revenge. For Sim's death and Pastor Price as well.

(Chapter 29)

(The Demon's Domain)

The team was now using this new attitude and raw energy for fuel. To make them all ready for battle with this intense Demon. The Lightning was now flashing so bright. As it came out of the sky. Looming just over top of the Rogers Farm land. It had a super spooky look about it now. Not like it had been the first time around. They now knew the Demon was trying to put fear into them once again.

Trying to take them all out of their element. Before the next battle had even begun. Tracey got on her radio and told the group to be ready. To not allow this entity to scare them in any way. She reassured the whole team that they could in fact do this. And that she didn't doubt them in any way what so ever. She told them. "Let's hit this Demon right on the chin". "And put his ass down for the count for good".

The team pulled back onto the Rogers Farm land just at the right time. The storm was right over top of them now. That was the key part of the whole thing. The evil would come out to play for sure. More during a storm than on any another night. And that was needed in order for a victory to take place. As they pulled in they jumped out and pulled their gear quickly.

They wanted to jump in full force and catch this thing while it was not as strong. With fear came power and as the fear grew in them so did the power in the beast. They all ran into the house and set up cameras and headed down to the basement pouring Holy water as they went. Coming back upstairs the team immediately headed up to the second floor. Sprinkling the blessed water as they traveled.

As they all headed down the steps their it was in that moment. The sounds of the hooves could be heard yet once again. Coming their way and fast. Tracey yelled at everyone to jump off of the stairs as fast as possible. They all dove and hit the living room floor. Now the whole team was filthy as they had landed in soot and burnt remnants from the fire. That were strung out, all along the floor.

(Chapter 30)

(The Demon's Domain)

The team had totally upset the Demon something fierce now. As they got up off of the wet floor of the living room. Every Book that had been on the book shelf had now flown off towards them all at once. Then one by one they each caught fire. But didn't burn for long. The water had drenched them immensely. Keeping them from burning at a normal pace. As the little fires of each book slowly burnt out.

"See what I said team" Tracey yelled at her group. As she were now excited for the first time. "We got this son of a bitch" she yelled out yet again. "Now let's bless this first floor and be gone". Tracey said as she finished her motivational rant. The team stayed tight together as they blessed the rest of the house. Running through each room as fast as they could.

They could only hear the hooves of the Demon running around in the hallway of the second floor. The team had just finished blessing the kitchen with the Holy water. They stepped back into the living room. The Demons hooves were pounding the wood of the floor in the hallway. As it traveled back and forth now. As if it were a little bit confused on what to do next.

Then the house went silent all of a sudden. Out of nowhere fire blew up and out of the floor vents throughout the entire house. Then the lights all seemed to flash over as sparks flew from the ceiling lights. The loudest growl came shortly after that. They had managed to really upset this beast from the depths of hell. And it was letting them know just how badly they had done so.

Now even though the Demon seemed to be mad as fire. Not one member of the team had been harmed this time around. The only thing left to do was bless the living room. Where the activity seemed to be strong. The group blessed the room quickly. Then in that moment Tracey said. "Everyone out of the house right now". The team all prepared for the exit.

The house started to shake as if their was an Earthquake taking place. The Ceiling fans all fell to the floor in an instant. Mike ran immediately towards the window and dove out and onto the front porch. He then headed towards the front door. As he got to the door it wouldn't open. So he stepped back and kicked it with all of his might.

(Chapter 31)

(The Demon's Domain)

But with no luck the door would still not open. All of a sudden Arron came flying out of the window. Crashing onto the front porch. Mike yelled to his brother quickly. "Help me now". As they both kicked the door knocking it off of the hinges. Sheriff Landers came out first. Then last but not least Tracey appeared. "Get the hell off of this porch" she yelled out to the team.

The group all ran and jumped from the porch. As they all hit the yard. They all looked towards the house. It was falling to pieces slowly but surely. Growls could be heard from the Demon now. And it was very upset in that moment. It had been somewhat defeated by the same team it had just pushed out of the house not long ago. Earlier that morning.

Then silence came as the house stopped shaking. The scene was that of a Tornado or better yet a Hurricane. Debris was laying everywhere now. Wood and Books soot from the earlier fire. Glass from the windows being shattered by the Demon and the fire also. It just looked like a war movie had been shot there on location. "Well" Tracey said. "Atleast there is a house still standing". She calmly said.

"Yes" the Sheriff replied. "I'm sure without a doubt in my mind". "The family will rebuild and start over". "I've known them for years". He stated. There was no doubt that the family were strong willed. To have to deal with the craziness that had now been going on for quite some time now. The question that now remained was if in fact the team had managed to cast out the Demon. Once and for all ?

With confidence the team now gathered together in a small group. As they hugged one another. Showing love and appreciation for each other. They all took one last look at the house. And then all headed towards their vehicles. They all shook the Sheriff's hand before leaving to get in their cars and head towards home. Finally it was over and time to plan for the next mission.

(Chapter 32)

(The Demon's Domain)

As the team drove now towards home. They all talked about the wildness they had all just experienced. The investigation had been without any doubts one of the toughest they had ever done. They all wondered though in all honesty. If they had really defeated the evil from within that home. Then the question was asked by the boss Tracey.

She asked both of the Brothers if they would go back with her. If the family ever called back and needed help once again. The brothers both replied back to their boss in an instant. "Absolutely" they both said. "We will go anywhere with you Tracey" They both said with confidence. "But we will need to add a few members to our team first Boss". Mike said as he lowered his head in sadness over the loss of Sims.

Arron said to his brother as he looked back at him from the front seat of the car. "I know your hurting brother" Arron said to his brother. "I know he was a great friend to you Mikey". Arron said sadly. "We will feel his loss from here on out". "He will never be replaced" Tracey said proudly. "He was a great Investigator".

Mike replied back to them both in that moment. "Yes" "he was great in the field". "And he was also a superior teammate as well. "I will miss my friend deeply". The team continued to make the drive home.

So they could regroup and also bury their fallen team member. Then they would take the proper time
out. In order to heal from their immense loss.

Tracey would give a Mike a month out of respect. To allow him to grieve and mourn the loss of his best
friend. They had grown up together and had spent most of their childhood together. The bond was
certainly a deep one. And she knew this loss was not something one just gets over and moves on from.
Tracey would need Mike at his best. Before she would even feel comfortable in doing another
investigation.

(Chapter 33)

(The Demon's Domain)

Then and only then would they be ready to handle the next investigation. They all had come to the
acceptance of the fact. That they may have to go right back out to the Rogers Farm. And once again

battle the Demon that they'd just faced. If the call was made they surely wouldn't back down from this evil they were now well familiar with.

That would without a doubt help the team go in with a much needed confidence. That would most definetly be needed. If they stood any chance of beating the Demons again. But if this were to happen again. The team was dead set on going back out to the farm. And beating this evil back down to the depths of Hell. Where they had come from in the very beginning.

(The End)

(Written By Jeffrey Lilly)

(August 18th 2022)

Thanks to the Zombie Media Publishing Team. And as well as the Crypto Crew.

I dedicate this Book to my Sons. My boys have motivated me to be my very best. In order for me to leave a legacy behind. I am trying to do at this moment in time. As I write each of my books from deep down inside my soul. For the Kids and the adults as well to read. Hoping to just give one person the hope that is needed. To change their lives for the better.

www.ingramcontent.com/pod-product-compliance
Lightning Source LLC
Chambersburg PA
CBHW060217120726
48004CB00008B/1853